The ADVENTURES of PROVIDENCE TRAVELER
—1503—

Uh-Oh, Leonardo!

WRITTEN AND ILLUSTRATED

by

ROBERT SABUDA

ATHENEUM BOOKS *for* YOUNG READERS
NEW YORK LONDON TORONTO SYDNEY SINGAPORE

Providence Traveler liked to make things.

Not simple things like macaroni pictures or tinfoil crowns. Providence made things that had never been made before. She built a Drip-Drop Alarm Clock that dumped a cup of water on your head if you didn't wake up when it went off. The Automatic Dinner Reducer shoveled olives (which Providence hated) under her plate when no one was looking. Providence always kept a small sketchbook in her pocket. "Just in case I have an idea," she said.

Most of all, Providence had a hero. He wasn't a movie star or a race-car driver. Providence's hero was Leonardo da Vinci, the Italian artist and inventor who had lived hundreds of years ago. She had checked out of the library every single book about Leonardo at least three times. Providence slowly turned the pages and marveled at his inventions. She even made small wooden models of many of the designs. Soon Providence knew everything there was to know about each invention he had designed and how it worked.

Except one.

Once, at the library, when she was reaching for her favorite book, *Leonardo da Vinci: Boy, Was He Busy*, an old piece of dusty paper slid from the shelf. The page was covered with a strange drawing of a large mouse made of wood. The mouse had a key coming out of its back. On the front of the mouse was a small panel with numbers and a large globe beside a tiny arrow. Below the drawing were detailed instructions for building the mouse. But what was it? A date at the bottom of the page read 1504. Providence quickly realized Leonardo da Vinci must have made the drawing himself, and the only way to figure out what it did was to make it.

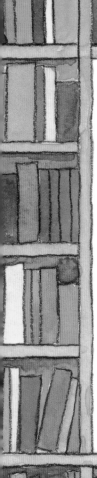

For many days Providence excitedly followed the instructions on the piece of paper. She had to hold the paper up to a mirror, since Leonardo always wrote his notes backward.

To keep them a secret, she thought.

Although the mouse appeared simple on the outside, the inside was filled with complicated wooden gears, levers, and pulleys. Four powerful magnets went into the globe. Providence placed several wooden whistles, flutes, and a small paper bellows inside the head. Each one made a different sound when air whispered through it.

Just when she was almost finished, her younger brother, Malcolm, burst into the room, followed closely by their next-door neighbors, the McMuzzin twins.

"The amazing, stupendous, and unbelievable Malcomini will now perform his final and greatest illusion," Malcolm pronounced to the twins. To Providence he whispered, "I've been practicing this one for weeks."

Providence chuckled and went down to the basement to get one last piece of wood. When she returned she saw Malcolm's feet sticking straight up out of a large cardboard box in the center of her room. From inside the box, she heard him muttering, "The frog is supposed to disappear! Disappear! It says so right in the book."

Then Providence saw with horror that the McMuzzin twins were each standing on one side of the wooden mouse, furiously winding the key at its back.

Before she could stop them, the globe in the center of the mouse began to spin wildly. A steady humming noise filled the air.

"NO!" she cried, and rushed forward, tipping over the box Malcolm was in. Malcolm and the box tumbled into the twins, who fell, knocking over the wooden mouse. There was a loud crack like thunder, and the room exploded in a flash of bright light.

The next thing Providence knew, they were outside.

"Wow, now THAT'S a trick," said Malcolm, sitting up in the grass.

Providence heard a whirring noise next to her. The wooden mouse lay on its side. Its globe had stopped spinning, and the numbers in the panel read: +1503.

The mouse slowly turned its head and let out a low whistle. Providence carefully propped it up on its feet and looked around.

Their house was gone, their street was gone, the entire neighborhood was gone. They were at the top of a grassy hill with a river at the bottom and a strange city in the distance.

"That big building with the dome on it looks familiar," she said.

Providence turned back to the wooden mouse and examined its globe. The small arrow was pointing at the country of Italy. They must be in Italy! "That's Florence Cathedral," she whispered. "But how could that be? The city of Florence is in Italy!"

When Providence turned back for a second look, she gasped. Running toward the city were two figures who looked familiar.

"Oh, no," moaned Providence, "the McMuzzin twins! We can't lose them!"

After running halfway down the hill, Providence heard a
WHOOSH as the largest bird she had ever seen passed closely
over their heads.

"AAAAAAAAAAAHHHHHHHHHHHHHHHHHH!" the
bird screeched as it crashed into the ground, flinging grass and
dirt everywhere.

The enormous bird rocked back and forth. Then suddenly a
terrible beast leaped out of it. The beast thrashed its monstrous
head back and forth. It began to scream and bellow. "IT DOESN'T
WORK! IT STILL DOESN'T WORK!"

Then Providence realized it wasn't the head of a beast at all but some kind of strange mask that almost looked like a helmet with goggles. Underneath it was an ordinary but very angry mouse with wild hair.

"Time after time I fall from the sky like a stone!" he ranted. "How can I become a bird if I can't leave the nest?"

Noticing the mechanical mouse, he shouted, "What is this? *Topo di legno?* A mouse of wood?" The frightening figure stepped closer, his eyes burning with curiosity. He reached out with dirty, grass-stained paws like the wicked witch in a fairy tale.

"Run!" screamed both Providence and Malcolm.

They hurried toward a weathered stone bridge with the old mouse howling at them to bring the *topo* back.

The bridge took them across a river and into the city. The streets were narrow and ran through closely packed houses and shops. All the residents of the town seemed to be dressed as if they were going to a costume party.

"What is going on here?" whispered Malcolm.

Providence hurried them along. Where were the twins? They had to find them. She noticed the residents of the city staring at their clothes, which must have seemed odd to them.

Providence spotted a maid setting a basket of laundry outside a doorway.

"Come on," Providence whispered, and raced toward the basket. She threw a large, floppy hat on Malcolm, a plain one on herself, and an enormous dress on the wooden mouse. As Providence was lacing up the back of the dress, she made a terrible discovery. "Your key! It's gone!"

Providence thought back. The twins had wound up the mouse with the key, there had been a flash, and now they were in Florence, Italy. The key must provide the power for the wooden mouse, just like in a windup clock. The twins must have the key! If they were ever going to get back home, they had to find the twins.

The Streets of Florence

sketches by
Providence
Traveler

Beautifully carved marble statues are everywhere.

Fountain

Wealthy ladies never go out into the streets without an attendant.

High-heeled shoes to prevent muddy dress

Pickpocket!

Arguing scholars discuss all the news of the day (and loudly, too!).

Nuns

Priest

Beggar

Members of the church provide for the poor, sick, and orphaned children.

Kids playing *civettino* or "little owl." You try to avoid being hit while keeping your foot in contact with your opponent's.

Gold florin

Peppercorns

Eels

Scale

Ginger and cloves

Cinnamon

Carp

Trout

Banking is done at the money changers. The florin is the most valuable coin in all of Europe.

Spices are a luxury and, besides adding flavor to a meal, are often used to preserve food.

Because Florence is not near the sea, most fish come from lakes or streams. Eels, yuk!

Sponges   Jewelry
Candles

Ink   Quills   Paper

Candied   Medicinal
orange   herbs
rinds

The apothecary shop sells just about
everything for the home (even secret
potions said to make hair grow!).

Clothes
for sale

Scissors   Damask   Silk
(woven   Wool
design)

Woolen cloth from Florence is
the best in all of Italy and
provides jobs for thousands.

Air-dried   Vent
macaroni

Oven

rolling   Ravioli   Bread
out
lasagne

All pasta is made by hand
and bread is baked
fresh every day.

Writing the
marriage
contract

Ring

A marriage ceremony. Brides are usually
between the ages of fourteen and sixteen!

Bad disguises
No key

Us looking for the twins.

My pencil

My sketchbook

Asparagus
Artichoke
Eggplant

Fennel

Beans   Onion   Garlic

Potato

A farmer sells vegetables
directly from his cart.
No olives today,
thank goodness!

Eggs   Strainer

Dry   Wet
cheese ricotta
cheese

Eggs and cheese come directly
from the farm because they
spoil so quickly.

Strawberries
Raisins   Sour oranges
and lemons
(very expensive)

Grapes Cherries Almond Walnuts
milk

Apples Melons   Pears

Fresh fruit is only available in
warmer seasons. Nuts are
eaten as snacks.

Racing around a corner, Providence collided with a towering figure, knocking them both off their feet.

"Bishop Strozzi! Are you all right?" an attendant asked, helping the elegantly dressed mouse to his feet.

"I'm *so* sorry," stammered Providence. "I mean—"

"Hmph!" interjected the bishop, casting a steely eye at the wooden mouse. "What is THAT?" He began to examine the mouse more closely. "Why, this unholy monstrosity appears to be a mechanical—"

"THERE YOU ARE!" came a voice from behind them. Hurrying up the street was the old mouse, still covered with grass.

"MY ANGELS!" he cried, winking at Providence. "And my magnificent *topo*! I've been looking everywhere for you! You've given me quite a scare, as I'm sure I did to you earlier. Now come along and stop bothering the busy church mice."

"You should teach those youngsters to respect their elders, Maestro," the bishop called after them. "After all, this isn't the Dark Ages, it's 1503!"

The old mouse smiled weakly at the bishop and nudged them quickly back into the crowd. "You must be careful," he warned. "The bishop is one of the most unhappy fellows in Florence. He doesn't like science or things that are not naturally of this world, especially new devices he can't understand. And he certainly wouldn't understand about your *topo* here." Their new friend peered carefully at the wooden mouse. "Why, even I don't understand!"

They came to a house on a small, narrow street and started in. Next to the door frame was a brass plate engraved with the words: INVENTOR AT WORK. PLEASE KNOCK LOUDLY.

Providence was amazed at all the rooms filled with tools, pieces of wood in various shapes and sizes, painting supplies, canvases, and all manner of strange-looking contraptions. Who was this "inventor at work"?

The old mouse took them upstairs, where his housekeeper brought them a fine lunch.

"Ah," he gushed, "my favorites, green olive soup and black olive lasagne!"

Providence gritted her teeth. If only she had her Automatic Dinner Reducer.

"So, my young visitors, I can tell you are not from this city," said the bearded mouse, "and the last time I checked, mice who walked were not made of wood, am I right, Topo?"

Providence was about to answer when she noticed a small notebook lying open on the table. The notes it contained were written backward.

"Leonardo da Vinci," Providence whispered excitedly. She smiled, but wondered. If Leonardo had designed Topo, why didn't he recognize his own invention? Then it occurred to her. The instructions she had followed to build Topo were dated 1504. This was 1503. Leonardo hadn't invented Topo yet.

"Come," said Leonardo, slurping down the last of his soup. "We must go check up on my workshop."

In Leonardo's Workshop

Besides being an inventor, Leonardo is a famous painter!

Linen canvas can be stretched across a frame to paint on.

Wood panels made from poplar, oak, or silver fir trees are perfect for painting on.

Charcoal sticks are used for sketching. Pencils haven't been invented yet.

Walnut or linseed oil is added to the pigments to turn them into paint.

Walnuts

Flax plant

Flaxseed is crushed to make linseed oil.

The fur or hair from animals is used to make brushes.

Gesso, a soft mineral, is mixed with water and brushed onto the panel or canvas before painting.

Pestle

Mortar

Pigments are crushed into powder using a mortar and pestle.

Cochineal beetles are crushed to make "carmine" or red.

Buckthorn berries are crushed to make "yellow lake" or yellow.

Lapis lazuli, a rare stone, is crushed to make "ultramarine" or blue.

sketches by
Providence Traveler

No nails. Dovetail joints.

Mannequins with plaster-covered clothes are used as models for sketching.

An assistant or apprentice places a crisscross frame on the back of a paneled painting to support it.

Paper funnel

Canvas is stretched over a frame and secured with nails.

Gesso is applied to make a smooth painting surface.

Pigments are carefully crushed. (They're expensive!)

The colors are separated into different bowls.

Angry client

Apologetic apprentice

Sometimes apprentices help finish the paintings because Leonardo is so busy.

Leonardo is often late finishing projects. Sometimes he never finishes them all!

Storage chest

Many workshops also create statues, armor, and painted furniture.

Providence could hardly believe she was talking with Leonard da Vinci! She explained about the construction of the mouse, the accident in her room when the mouse was wound up, but most importantly about the key and the missing twins.

"Do not worry," promised Leonardo, "we'll find your key and friends."

Then he touched Topo, his eyes growing wide. "So this wooden mouse has brought you here from another time? And you say I designed it? Incredible! You must be very clever indeed to have constructed it," he said to Providence, "because all the things I build never seem to work!" Providence smiled and began to blush.

"What exactly was that supposed to do?" Malcolm asked, pointing to the large cloth-covered device that Leonardo had crashed on the hill.

"Oh, it does nothing," moaned Leonard, "absolutely nothing. I have been working on it for years. It is supposed to allow one to fly, yet fails each time."

Providence already knew from her books what the problem with the flying machine was. It was made of wood, leather, and cow horn—materials that are too heavy for flying. Unless the mouse strapped into the machine was incredibly powerful, Leonardo's dream would never take flight.

"I have the perfect solution to help us find your lost twins," beamed Leonardo, changing the subject. "We shall make POSTERS! I have a good friend who prints books using the latest techniques. He can even print an actual drawing onto the paper! We shall make posters of your twins and place them around the city!"

They set off down the street again and soon arrived at a very busy and noisy workshop where they were met by a small, wiry mouse with ink-stained hands.

"Filippo!" called Leonardo. "Your old friend needs a favor from the best printer in all of Florence!"

Providence described what the McMuzzin twins looked like to Leonardo, who drew up a sketch. Then Filippo redrew the sketch onto a block of wood and began to carve away the areas that wouldn't be printed.

While he was carving, Providence and Malcolm wandered around the workshop.

Filippo's Print Shop
sketches by Providence Traveler

Books can be bought here but are very expensive. Readers treasure their home libraries as if they were gold.

Cutting tools

All the wood that is cut away won't print.

Sharp tools are used to cut away areas from the block of wood with Leonardo's sketch on it.

Each metal letter is backward.

Drying pages

Blank paper

Printed pages

The typesetter arranges each letter into a word. The words become sentences until all the text on the page is "set."

The proofreader checks the spelling and makes sure the printing isn't messy.

Turpentine

Lampblack, a fine, black soot

Ink is made from lampblack, linseed oil, and turpentine (It stinks!). The ink isn't a liquid but more like a thick paste.

Sometimes red ink is used for printing, but any other colorful decoration has to be painted on each page by hand.

Wood screw

Bar to turn screw

Ink ball

Paper

Tympan

PRINTING THE POSTER

The cut wood block and the typeset letters, now called a form, are placed on the press. Ink is spread on the form. A piece of paper is attached to the tympan and then flipped onto the inked form.

Turning the screw

Big muscles

Platen

The form and the tympan are slid beneath the heavy platen. The screw is turned and the platen presses the paper onto the inked form.

The platen is slid back out and the paper is removed. Two-hundred-and-fifty sheets of paper can be printed in one hour.

Hard work!

Twins!

The printed poster!

Providence was so excited when the posters were finished. Rushing toward the door she turned to wave good-bye to Filippo and ran straight into another mouse coming into the workshop.

"Bishop Strozzi!" cried Filippo.

"Well, if it isn't the three blind mice again," said the bishop, glaring at Providence, Malcolm, and Topo.

He turned to Filippo. "I'm here to see a copy of your newly printed Bible." The bishop noticed one of Leonardo's posters lying on the floor and picked it up.

"*Maestro* da Vinci, it appears you have finally chosen a useful career. Congratulations. Perhaps you should have made some pretty posters for this evening's Feast celebration as well."

He turned to Topo. "Then you would not waste time on creations such as this. A device that struts around as if it were living? What other evil tricks does it perform?"

Leonardo quickly stepped between the bishop and Topo. "Why, this is just one of my assistants in costume for Carnival tonight," the inventor replied. "He's riding on one of the floats. Say hello . . . uh . . . Peppino."

Topo looked horrified and whistled a small peep.

The bishop glared at Leonardo.

"Oh, my . . . uh . . . Peppino has a terrible cold. He's practically lost his voice. Take care, Your Grace, not to catch it!"

The bishop quickly stepped backward.

"He just needs his key to feel better," Malcolm blurted out helpfully.

"Key?" the bishop asked suspiciously. "What key?"

"Well, thank you so much for the posters, Filippo," interrupted Leonardo. "We'll see you at the celebration this evening."

Leonardo, Providence, Malcolm, and Topo spent the rest of the afternoon putting up posters throughout the entire city. By the time they returned to Leonardo's studio, everyone was very tired, especially Topo.

Providence knew that the time-traveling mouse needed to be wound up again soon. She was afraid that if they didn't find the key, it would shut down completely. Over a light supper of olive casserole, she spoke up. "Maestro da Vinci, thank you so much for your help and hospitality, but I'm afraid we really must continue looking for the twins."

Leonardo pulled on his beard thoughtfully.

"Tonight at the Feast of Saint Giovanni," he said, "all of

Florence will be out celebrating and surely someone will have seen the posters and found the twins. We will all go together. Agreed?"

Leonardo quickly made up costumes for them out of the clothing his models wore when he was painting them.

Providence and Malcolm smiled their approval and turned to Topo. Topo sat in the chair, eyes closed, completely still, frozen in time.

Leonardo did his best to cheer them up. "Be strong," he said. "You are truly the youth of the Renaissance: bold, brave, and determined."

Providence didn't feel brave. She felt worried. If they couldn't find the twins, what would they do? They could be stuck in this time and place forever! She tried not to think about it as they stepped out into the street and became part of the celebration to honor Saint Giovanni.

The Feast of St. Giovanni
sketches by Providence Traveler

Every June, St. John the Baptist, the patron saint of Florence, is honored with a lavish celebration.

Citizens wear their best clothes to show off the wealth of Florence.

Silk banners or *palii* are raised high. Lilies, the city flower, top the poles.

Papier-mâché statue

Moses parting the sea

Silk waves

Acrobat

Juggler

Entertainment is everywhere!

I've never seen so many floats in *my* life!

| Roast onion salad | Mushrooms with spices | Chickpea soup | Poached eggs in custard | Sweet-and-sour trout | Eel pie | Cherry pudding | Marzipan treats | Whole-pear pie | Apple-jelly candies |

Leonardo wasn't joking when he called it a feast!

An enormous canopy of beautiful cloth called *cielo* or heaven is sewn together and placed over the entire plaza.

A poetry contest

Bad poem

Fireworks!

Me still looking for the twins

Selling wine. Water in Florence is not clean enough to drink.

Trumpet

Drum

Lute

Leonardo has a beautiful singing voice.

Olive costume. Yuk!

A popular style of music is called madrigal, which is usually romantic or funny.

The city of Florence bustled with excitement. Citizens cheered and applauded as the floats portraying biblical scenes and religious legends rolled through the narrow streets and out into the plaza.

One of the floats depicted Saint George slaying the dragon. The dragon was a two-headed creature with a very long tail. For some reason the tip of the tail looked familiar to Providence. Then she realized it was the rounded end of a large key. Topo's key! And the dragon's heads were the heads of the twins!

Providence leaped up onto a wheel of the float, landed with a **THUMP** on the hard platform, and stumbled toward the two-headed monster. "You're safe!" she cried out, reaching for the giggling twins. Then she herself was shoved backward by a strong arm.

Saint George towered over her, his silver helmet ablaze with the reflection of fireworks.

"I wouldn't try that if I were you," boomed Saint George. "These poor, poor youngsters are now officially orphans. Someone responsible must care for them and their *only* possession." He grabbed Topo's key and stood next to the twins.

Saint George lifted his visor and from within his helmet, Bishop Strozzi's face smiled wickedly.

"Do you really think I'm so easily fooled?" he sneered. "I know this key has something to do with that mechanical monstrosity, that unholy *topo di legno*. Crazy, old Leonardo's devices are a danger and fill everyone's head with wild ideas. So if this key holds the secret to his wicked creature, then you will NEVER get it back!"

Suddenly there was another **THUMP** on the float as an angel seemed to fly over Providence and land directly in front of the bishop.

"The amazing, stupendous, and unbelievable Malcomini will now perform his greatest and final illusion!"

Malcolm threw his cape over the twins just as the bishop was reaching down to grab him. "DISAPPEAR!" he commanded.

When he lifted his cape, the twins were still there.

But the key in the bishop's hand was gone.

The bishop roughly pushed Malcolm aside. He stumbled against Providence, who fell off the float, her sketchbook slipping out from her belt.

"WHERE IS THAT KEY?!" the bishop screamed, searching frantically.

Malcolm let his cape gently slide over the edge of the float.

It hit the street with a CLUNK . . . and out rolled the key.

Providence snatched it up and raced past the approaching Leonardo, calling out, "I won't be long!"

"But the celebration ends at the cathedral soon," he yelled back. "You'll never make it through the crowds."

The bishop picked up the twins and pulled the young magician down off the float. Malcolm grabbed Providence's sketchbook just before the bishop tied his hands together with his own cape. Then he shoved his way past Leonardo and headed toward the cathedral with his captives.

Inside Florence Cathedral by Malcolm

Holy picture

Columns to
hold up roof

Saint's tooth,
a Holy
Relic

Candles for the
celebration can
weigh almost
one hundred
pounds!

It took over one hundred and
forty years to build the cathedral.

People come to pray
up to three times a day.

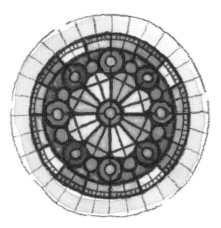

Music filled the soaring heights of the cathedral. At the rear, glorious circular stained-glass windows bathed the celebrants in warm colors.

Bishop Strozzi, his face still flushed with anger, had made his way to the cathedral and changed into his official robes. He strode to the front, where Malcolm and the twins were well hidden, unseen by the congregation.

The music came to an end, and the bishop opened his mouth to speak.

WHOOSH, WHOOSH, WHOOSH.

The bishop looked up in annoyance.

WHOOSH, WHOOSH, WHOOSH.

Outside, the noise grew louder and louder.

WHOOSH, WHOOSH, WHOOSH.

As the crowd looked around curiously, the sound became almost deafening.

WHOOSH, WHOOSH, WHOOSH.

A great shadow fell across the face of one of the stained-glass windows. For a moment, everything in the church became completely still.

CRRRASSSHHHH! The window exploded in a shower of glittering colors as Providence flew through on the back of Topo. The wooden mouse was strapped into Leonardo's flying machine and was flapping its arms and legs furiously.

The crowd gasped. Maestro da Vinci's flying machine worked!

"There they are!" Providence yelled, pointing down. Topo dipped one of the machine's wings, knocking the bishop to the floor while Providence scooped up Malcolm and the twins.

"The front door!" Providence shouted to Topo. "Get us out of here!" But the wooden mouse had used up most of its energy making the machine fly. Topo flew halfway through the cathedral, then skidded to a stop near the front door. The huge crowd rushed over, bubbling with excitement.

"LET ME THROUGH!" howled Bishop Strozzi. He tried unsuccessfully to push his way through all of the admirers. "STEP ASIDE, I SAY, RIGHT THIS INSTANT! This *topo di legno* is a deception! It is all a trick of Leonardo's!"

"A trick?" shouted Leonardo, rushing in and trying to catch his breath. "Is it a trick when we use our minds to observe and study and create? This magnificent device shows us what we can do if we follow our dreams. And dreams only become real with the help of others. Perhaps we should show our appreciation to my brave young assistants!"

While the crowd cheered wildly, Providence untied Malcolm, who ran around the back of Topo and began winding the key. She changed the date in the small display to their own time and rotated the globe until their home location was next to the tiny arrow. Providence picked up the twins and grabbed on to Topo. "It flew," she whispered to Leonardo.

"It flew," he said, smiling back, "because of you."

A steady humming began to come from Topo, and the globe started to spin.

"NOOOOOO!" Bishop Strozzi raged, his voice echoing throughout the cathedral. "Whose going to pay for that *windooooow?!*"

There was a bright flash, and then they were gone.

When Providence sat up, the first thing she felt was the giggling twins scurrying past her into the living room. Malcolm lay on the floor snoring loudly, his glasses askew, his cape covering him like a blanket.

Topo stood in the corner, silent and uncomplaining.

Providence crawled into her bed. She looked up at a small model of Leonardo's flying machine hanging on its string. In a few moments she, too, fell asleep, and her gentle breathing spun the model around and around and around.

From the early 1300s to the late 1500s, after the harshness and suffering of the Dark Ages, Europe enjoyed a revival of learning and the arts. This new period became known as the "Renaissance," after the French word "rebirth." Tradition gave way to curiosity as explorers like Christopher Columbus set sail for the unknown and proved the world was round. Merchants became rich because of increased ocean trade. More people left the countryside to live in cities where knowledge and education were prized above all else.

And the most exciting place to be when the Renaissance began was Italy. Florence, the richest state at that time, was as the center of the artistic revolution.

Dominated politically by a powerful family of bankers, the Medici, and the wealth of the Catholic Church, many great works of art were commissioned.

Artists like famed sculptor Michelangelo Buonarroti and the architect responsible for the magnificent dome of Florence's cathedral, Filippo Brunelleschi, brought artistic vision to new heights. Artists investigated and represented the world as they truly saw it.

Born in 1452, Leonardo da Vinci spent a lifetime observing the world around him and filled some six thousand pages of notebooks that have survived to this day. Leonardo wrote backward because he was left-handed. Writing this way prevented the wet ink from smudging. When he really wanted to keep his notes a secret, he wrote in code.

Dreams and ideas led Leonardo to design musical instruments, stage sets, cranes (used to lift heavy objects), war machines (tanks and machine guns), canal systems, a primitive automobile, a bicycle, a heating system for a duchess's bathtub, and even a water alarm clock that pulled a stick tied to the sleeper's foot.

Although best known as a painter, Leonardo created very few finished works. To improve his art, he studied plants, flowers, animals, people, the flow of water, even dead bodies in a hospital, sketching everything in his notebooks. He was also an expert in sculpture, architecture, engineering, mathematics, and music, but his true passion was always drawing.

Leonardo loved animals and was a vegetarian, which was very unusual for the time. Quite popular and an excellent joke teller, he organized pageants and plays, selecting the music and even designing the costumes. He also created ingenious automatons, machines or toys that mimicked life after being wound up. Although he hoped his flying machine would soar like a bird, he actually based its design on the bat.

Leonardo died in 1519 at the age of sixty-seven.

For my fellow New Yorkers who got knocked down, but stood back up again

Atheneum Books for Young Readers
An imprint of Simon & Schuster Children's Publishing Division
1230 Avenue of the Americas
New York, New York 10020

Book design by Michael Nelson and Robert Sabuda
The text of this book is set in Deepdene.
The illustrations are rendered in pencil and watercolor.

Printed in Hong Kong
First Edition
2 4 6 8 10 9 7 5 3 1

LIBRARY OF CONGRESS CATALOGING-IN-PUBLICATION DATA
Sabuda, Robert.
Providence traveler 1503: Uh-oh, Leonardo! / Robert Sabuda.—1st ed.
p.   cm.
ISBN 0-689-81160-8
Summary: Providence the mouse travels through time to sixteenth-century Florence, Italy,
where she shares an adventure with Leonardo da Vinci, the inventor she admires so much.
[1.Leonardo, da Vinci, 14552-1519—Fiction. 2. Time travel—Fiction. 3. Inventors—Fiction.
4. Mice—Fiction. 5. Florence (Italy)—Fiction. 6. Italy—Fiction.]
Pz7.S1178 Pr 2003
[Fic]—dc21   2001041255